To Mia + Margot!

I Hope You Enjoy The Book. Let's Go Fishing Some Time!

For Ellery.
My little gator.

TWO GATORS
IN WADERS
by
Mark Maziarz

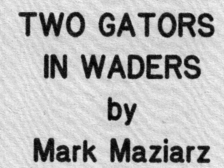

TWO BOLD EVERGLADERS, two Florida gators,
were bored of their place in the marsh.
They wanted some fun, where the clear rivers run,
and the sun's not so terribly harsh.

"How 'bout the Arctic?
It sounds pretty cool."
The little one said
to her dad.

"I was thinking of something
a little less frozen."
And he pulled a map he had.

"A fishing adventure
with freewheeling rivers,
fed from fresh waterfalls."

LITTLE FORK
Loveland, CO

Little Fork River known for its twisting rapids and clear water, the Little Fork River was first discovered by explorer and wildlife expert Archibald Von Twinkleton while studying the Great American Water Buffalo. Boasting twenty waterfalls, the river is a firshermen's paradise host to many fish species year round.

N
W   E
S

1 km   2km   5km

longitude _____ 00.10.01001N
latitude _____ 04.0000.37W
total elevation _____ 10,000000

"All we need
is some go-getter spirit
and these rubberized overalls."

So two gators in waders,
they said "catch ya later"
to the mangroves and the low hanging vines.
And they packed up their tackle,
and tied down their rods,
and took off with trout on their minds.

ARE WE THERE YET?
ARE WE THERE YET?
ARE WE THERE YET?
WERE NOT.
...and that's how it went
'til they were.

The river looked different
than the overgrown swamp,
and the crisp air made both of them "BRRR."

"So, this is the spot?" The little one asked.
"As sure as the sun," said Dad.
Then they unpacked their gear
and made their way down
to the Little Fork Riverhead.

They stepped to the water,
a dad and his daughter,
'til the stream came up
to their waists.

"And now here's the part where we pick out our flies.

CHECK OUT MY IMPECCABLE TASTE."

"There's the Parachute Adams.
It works in all seasons
and mimics a Mayfly quite well."

"And this Wooly Bugger
has a Maribou tail
and a body of tufted chenille."

"The Bunny Leech is sure to impress
with its rabbit fur and visual flair."

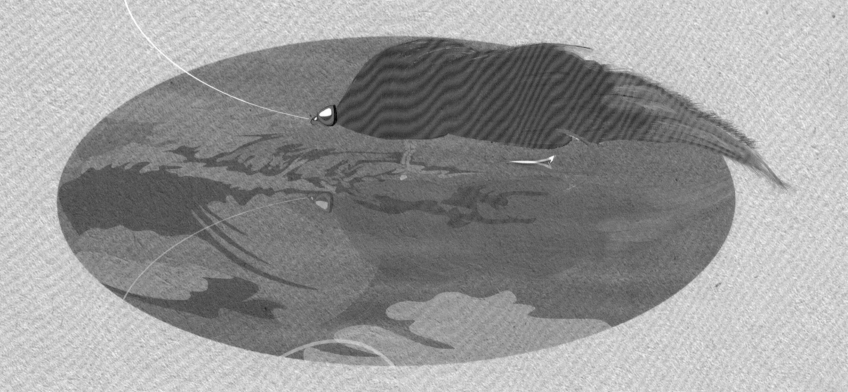

"And the Elk Hair Caddis
is a fave among anglers.
So is the Gold Ribbed Hare."

"IT'S CALLED THE GOLD RIBBED HARE'S EAR!
"THANKS! WE ARE DOING A WHOLE RHYMING THING!"
"OH GOTCHA! CARRY ON."

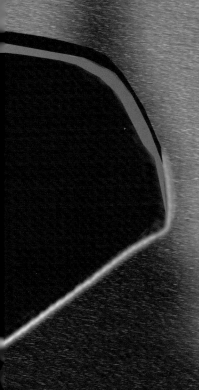

"The Pheasant Tail Nymph?
The Muddler Minnow?
Maybe the San Juan Worm?
They all can work magic
when the moment is right.
We should give them all a turn."

"And the Egg Sucking Leech
sounds a little bit gross,
but it just might land us a bass."

"The Disco Midge is tiny but tough
like somebody else I know.
And when temperatures drop,
it works like a champ.
So that might be the way to go."

"A Crayfish could work in water like this.
They mimic the native crustaceans.
So what's the play, little gator in waders?
After all, it's your vacation."

He looked up from his tackle
and couldn't believe
what had happened
during all of this time,

but a stringer of trout,
a day's catch, no doubt,
and another big lug on the line.

"Oh I chose mine,"
Said the gator in waders.
"and it works especially well.
It's got a tortilla chip body,
and wrapped around that
is a neon pink gummy worm tail."